DISNEY LEARNING
Everyday Stories

Be Mindful, Donald!

Written by Vickie Saxon • Illustrated by the Disney Storybook Artists
Special thanks to Dr. Renée Cherow-O'Leary

Lerner Publications ◆ Minneapolis

Lerner Publications Company
A division of Lerner Publishing Group, Inc.
241 First Avenue North
Minneapolis, MN 55401 USA

For reading levels and more information, look up this title at
www.lernerbooks.com.

Library of Congress Cataloging-in-Publication Data

The Cataloging-in-Publication Data for *Be Mindful, Donald! A Mickey &
Friends Story* is on file at the Library of Congress.
ISBN 978-1-5415-3255-7 (lib. bdg.)
ISBN 978-1-5415-3284-7 (pbk.)
ISBN 978-1-5415-3256-4 (eb pdf)

Manufactured in the United States of America
1-44847-35717-4/5/2018

It was a lovely morning in the neighborhood. The sun shone brightly in the blue sky, and the birds sang happily. Everything seemed wonderfully calm.

Inside Donald Duck's house, however, things were not quite so peaceful . . .

Splat! Donald flipped a pancake, and it landed on top of the refrigerator. He wanted to make a special breakfast for his nephews, but it wasn't easy.

"Aw, phooey!" Donald cried.

Huey, Dewey, and Louie burst noisily into the kitchen. "Morning, Uncle Donald!"

The boys piled their plates with food and ate their breakfast.

"Thanks, Uncle Donald!" they shouted. Then they ran outside to ride their bikes. They left behind quite a mess.

Donald was already tired, and the day had barely started!
Buzz, buzz! Donald took out his phone and saw a text from Daisy.
She was on vacation with her nieces, April, May, and June.
"It's busy here, taking care of all three girls at once! I can't keep
up with them. It reminds me to take time to be **mindful**," she wrote.

"Mindful?" Donald texted back. "What's that?"

"Start by being aware and grateful!" Daisy responded. "We're heading to the museum, so I'm turning off my phone. Have a great day!"

"Be aware of what?" Donald wondered.

Donald sighed. He had a lot of work to do. After he cleaned the kitchen, he went outside and started his weekend chores. He had to pull some weeds, mow the lawn, and paint the fence. He tried to do everything at once, but nothing went right. In his hurry, he even ran over a sprinkler with his lawn mower.

"Hey!" Donald sputtered as water sprayed everywhere.
Donald finally turned off the water, but his yard was a mess!
"Gee, I wish I could talk to Daisy. She would know what to do,"
he said to himself. He looked at her texts again and saw the
phrase "take time to be mindful."
Donald wished he understood what that meant!

Just then, Mickey called.

"Hiya, pal! Minnie and I will pick you up for our fishing trip in ten minutes," Mickey said.

"Oh no!" Donald gasped. "I totally forgot! My nephews are here this weekend."

"That's all right," said Mickey. "Goofy's going to take care of them, remember?"

Donald shook his head. He had forgotten about the fishing trip and about Goofy spending time with the boys. He really was trying to do too much at once!

"I'll be ready in a jiffy!" Donald told Mickey.

Donald smiled as he went to get his fishing gear.

"Oh boy, oh boy, oh boy!" he said. He couldn't wait to get to his favorite fishing spot.

Donald's friends arrived just as Huey, Dewey, and Louie returned from their bike ride.

"Hi, Goofy!" Huey called. "What are we gonna do today?"

"Why don't we start with a soccer game in the park?" Goofy suggested.

"Yay!" cheered the boys.

"Be good, boys. I'll bring back lots of fish, and we'll have a feast tomorrow," Donald said. He gave his nephews a **hug** before climbing into Mickey's car.

The moment Donald sat down, Pluto jumped into his lap and began licking his shirt.

"Pluto! What are you doing?" Mickey called out.

"He's eating pancake batter off my shirt!" said Donald.

Minnie giggled. "It looks like you had a rough morning," she said.

"Nothing seemed to go right today," Donald complained.

"I'm sorry to hear that," Minnie said.

"Let us know if we can help when we get back," Mickey added. "But for now, let's enjoy our trip."

As they drove through the country, Donald started to feel better. Maybe this fishing trip was just what he needed!

When they arrived at the lake, Minnie got out of the car
and began to **stretch**.

"Oh, it feels so good to stretch after that drive!" she said.
"You boys should stretch with me."

"What?!" Donald cried. He didn't want to stretch. He wanted
to catch fish!

"Give it a try," Minnie said. Together they all bent down low
and reached up high.

"I guess that does feel good," Donald admitted.

The friends climbed into a boat and pushed away from the shore.

"Aah, this is nice," Mickey said. He took a **deep breath**.

"Oh no!" Donald cried out. "I forgot to pack my fishing pole!"

"We can share," Minnie told him. "Besides, going fishing isn't just about catching fish."

"Yeah," Mickey agreed. "It's about enjoying the outdoors and spending time with your friends."

Donald had never thought this way about fishing before. He saw how much his friends were enjoying themselves and decided to follow their example. He breathed deeply, feeling the fresh air fill his lungs. He noticed the sunlight glinting off the water and realized how beautiful the lake was.

The friends took turns using the fishing poles, but no one caught any fish.

"Aw, phooey," Donald grumbled. "I promised the boys I'd bring back fish."

"They'll understand," Mickey said. "The fish just aren't biting today."

"I guess you're right," Donald sighed.

"Shh," Minnie suddenly said. "Do you hear that?"

Everyone stopped to **listen**. At first, Donald didn't hear anything. Then he closed his eyes and focused. He heard the gently lapping waves and the birdsong floating through the air. It was lovely.

When they got back to shore, they found a nice spot to spread out a blanket. Minnie decided to do some yoga while Mickey and Donald lay back to watch the clouds.

As they looked at the cloud shapes drifting slowly by, Donald said, "I really like being here. In fact, I **appreciate** being here."

Donald wondered if this is what Daisy meant when she talked about being mindful!

Soon it was time for their picnic. As the friends spread out the food, Donald's stomach growled. He was starving!

"The food looks great!" Donald said. He stuffed half a sandwich in his mouth.

Then he stopped. Things had gone wrong today when he'd tried to do them too quickly. When he **slowed down** and paid attention to what was happening, his day got better.

Donald took smaller bites and chewed slowly. He took time to enjoy his food.

The sun was setting by the time they finished their meal.

"Thanks for the delicious picnic and for the fishing trip,"
Donald told Mickey and Minnie. "I had a great time."

"Aw, shucks," Mickey said. "We had a great time too."

"Thanks for coming with us," Minnie added.

On the drive home, Donald watched the changing colors in
the sky. He stroked Pluto's soft fur, feeling peaceful and relaxed.

But when Donald got home, he walked in and saw a disaster!

The kitchen he had cleaned that morning was a mess again. Goofy, Huey, Dewey, and Louie had clearly had some accidents while making supper!

"Hiya, pals," Goofy said. "How was your fishing trip?"

"What . . . ? How . . . ? Why . . . ?" Donald was so shocked that he could barely talk!

Then Donald stopped and took a deep breath. He closed
his eyes and thought about his wonderful day at the lake. He
remembered what he had learned about being mindful.

"Come on, fellas! Time for a break!" Donald said. He led his
nephews and his friends outside. "We've all had a long day, so
let's take time to appreciate what a nice night it is."

Together, they looked up at the stars and
listened to the crickets. They breathed the night
air and smelled the clean scent of grass.

"It's nice to enjoy everything that's
happening right **here and now**,"
Donald said quietly.

Everyone agreed.

Later, they all helped clean up the kitchen.

"Thanks, everyone," Donald said.

"Anytime," his friends replied.

It was getting late, so Mickey, Minnie, Goofy,
and Pluto said their goodbyes.

Then Donald helped Huey, Dewey, and Louie get ready for bed. Donald tucked the boys in and read them a bedtime story.

"You're swell, Uncle Donald," said Huey as he yawned.

"Yeah, thanks, Uncle Donald," said Louie.

"G'night," Dewey said. Then he started to snore softly.

"Sleep well, boys," Donald whispered.

Donald walked quietly to the living room. He picked up his phone and texted Daisy one last note. "I hope you had a great day. I did! Thanks for reminding me to be mindful!"

Then he sat down in a comfy chair and sighed happily. He thought about everything that had happened and decided to work on being mindful every day.